ABOUT THE BANK STREET READY-TO-READ SERIES

Seventy years of educational research and innovative teaching have given the Bank Street College of Education the reputation as America's most trusted name in early childhood education.

Because no two children are exactly alike in their development, we have designed the *Bank Street Ready-to-Read* series in three levels to accommodate the individual stages of reading readiness of children ages four through eight.

- ○ *Level 1:* GETTING READY TO READ—read-alouds for children who are taking their first steps toward reading.
- ● *Level 2:* READING TOGETHER—for children who are just beginning to read by themselves but may need a little help.
- ○ *Level 3:* I CAN READ IT MYSELF—for children who can read independently.

Our three levels make it easy to select the books most appropriate for a child's development and enable him or her to grow with the series step by step. The *Bank Street Ready-to-Read* books also overlap and reinforce each other, further encouraging the reading process.

We feel that making reading fun and enjoyable is the single most important thing that you can do to help children become good readers. And we hope you'll be a part of Bank Street's long tradition of learning through sharing.

The Bank Street College of Education

To Julie and Karen
— B.B.

For Cody and Cooper
and the Town Hill Kids
— R.O.

THE FIGHT
A Bantam Little Rooster Book / November 1991

Little Rooster is a trademark of Bantam Books,
a division of Bantam Doubleday Dell Publishing Group, Inc.

Series graphic design by Alex Jay/Studio J
Editor: Gillian Bucky

Special thanks to James A. Levine, Betsy Gould, Sally Doherty,
Erin B. Gathrid, and Libby Ford.

Library of Congress Cataloging-in-Publication Data

Boegehold, Betty Virginia Doyle.
The fight.

(Bank Street ready-to-read)
''A Bantam little rooster book.''
''A Byron Preiss book.''
Summary: An accidental bump starts
a gigantic fight in the schoolyard,
where the students forget to use their
heads and use their fists instead.
ISBN 0-553-07086-X ISBN 0-553-35206-7 (pbk.)
[1. Schools—Fiction.   2. Stories in rhyme].
I. Oz, robin, ill.   II. Title.   III. Series.
PZ8.3.B59954Fi   1991
[E]
90-766

Published simultaneously in the United States and Canada

Bantam Books are published by Bantam Books, a division of Bantam Doubleday
Dell Publishing Group, Inc. Its trademark, consisting of the words ''Bantam Books''
and the portrayal of a rooster, is Registered in U.S. Patent and Trademark Office
and in other countries. Marca Registrada. Bantam Books, 666 Fifth Avenue, New
York, New York 10103.

PRINTED IN THE UNITED STATES OF AMERICA

0 9 8 7 6 5 4 3 2 1

Bank Street Ready-to-Read™

The Fight

by Betty D. Boegehold
Illustrated by Robin Oz

A Byron Preiss Book

A BANTAM LITTLE ROOSTER BOOK
NEW YORK · TORONTO · LONDON · SYDNEY · AUCKLAND

What do you think happened in the schoolyard?

This is Dan
who bumped into Fran,
which started the fight
in the schoolyard.

This is Will
being pushed by Fran,
who was bumped by Dan,
which started the fight
in the schoolyard.

This is Phil
being punched by Will,
who was pushed by Fran,
who was bumped by Dan,
which started the fight
in the schoolyard.

This is Lil
who was hit by Phil,
who he thought was Will,
who was pushed by Fran,
who was bumped by Dan,
which started the fight
in the schoolyard.

This is the teacher
named Mr. Hart,
who rushed to pull
the kids apart
and stop the fight
in the schoolyard.

This is the stone
sticking out of the ground
that tripped Mr. Hart
and spun him around.

Then Mr. Hart fell
into a swing.
The swing took off
like a living thing!

It gave Mr. Hart
the bumpiest ride,
before it dumped him
onto the slide!
Down, down, down
he went until—

This is the mound
that rose from the ground
with Lil and Phil,
as well as Will,
and Fran and Dan,
and Mr. Hart,
all in a pile
in the schoolyard.

This is the nurse
who heard the fuss.
This is the driver
who stopped his bus.

This is the crowd
that came on the run
to stop the fight
in the schoolyard.

These are the kids
they pulled apart,
and there they found
poor Mr. Hart
flat on the ground
in the schoolyard.

"It was Will!" said Phil.
"It was Phil!" cried Lil.
"It was Dan!" shouted Fran.
"It was dumb!" groaned Dan.
And then he said,
"I used my fists
and not my head!"

Phil said, "You're right.
This is a mess.
To top it off
we missed recess!"

One by one,
they did admit
they'd bumped and pushed
and punched and hit
until they forgot
what started it—

that silly fight in the schoolyard!